For my beautiful sons,
and our most amazing journey – G. Peter

For C & K – G. Parsons

PUFFIN BOOKS

UK | USA | Canada | Ireland | Australia | India | New Zealand | South Africa

Puffin Books is part of the Penguin Random House group of companies whose
addresses can be found at global.penguinrandomhouse.com.

www.penguin.co.uk
www.puffin.co.uk
www.ladybird.co.uk

Penguin
Random House
UK

First published 2020

001

Text copyright © Gareth Peter, 2020
Illustrations copyright © Garry Parsons, 2020

The moral right of the author and illustrator has been asserted

Printed in China

A CIP catalogue record for this book is available from the British Library

ISBN: 978–0–241–40577–2

All correspondence to:
Puffin Books, Penguin Random House Children's
One Embassy Gardens, New Union Square
5 Nine Elms Lane, London SW8 5DA

FSC
www.fsc.org
MIX
Paper from
responsible sources
FSC® C018179

My Daddies!

written by Gareth Peter   illustrated by Garry Parsons

PUFFIN

My daddies are amazing.
They're funny, kind and smart.

And when they
read me stories . . .

exciting journeys start . . .

Sometimes we battle **dragons**,

and find **treasure**
in their cave . . .

Then hunt for deadly dinosaurs . . .

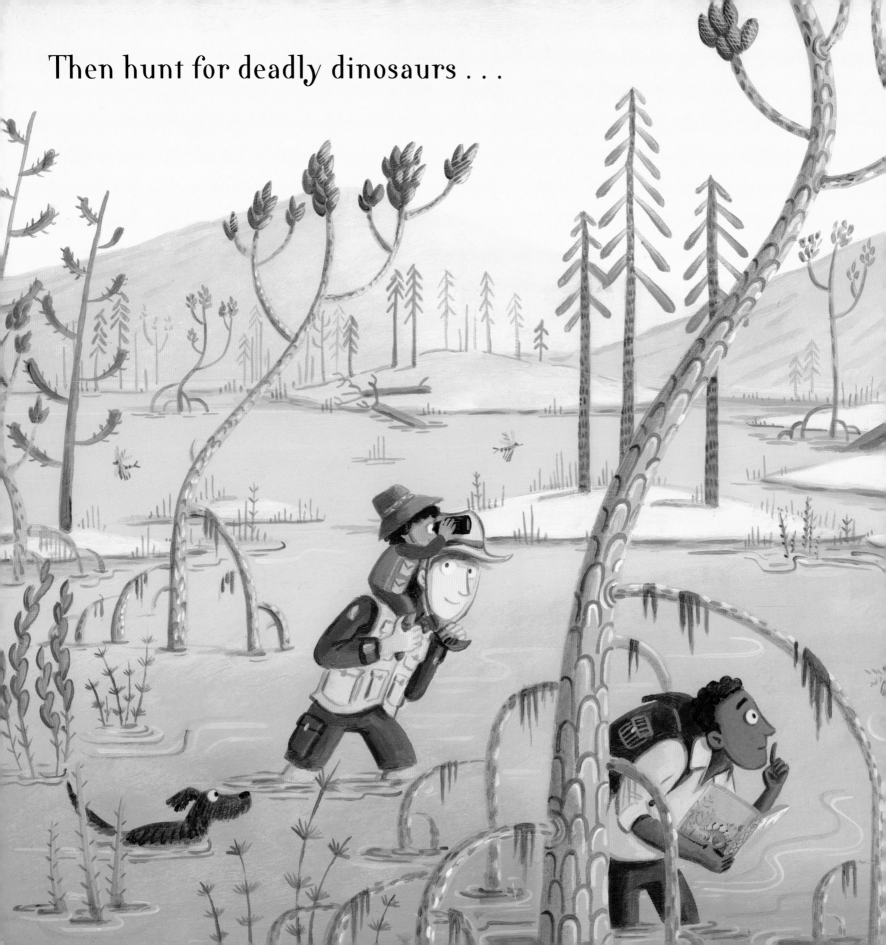

on days we're feeling brave!

Sometimes we build a rocket

and **blast off** to the moon . . .

Or sail to secret islands

and fly home in a balloon.

Books take us on these journeys
Over forest, sand and sea.
But my daddies' **favourite** story is . . .

. . . the one that brought them me!

MY Adoption
Story

Some children have two mummies,

and some, a mum and dad.

But I have **SUPER** daddies!

Who chose *me* . . .

I'm **SO** glad.

They're not the best at everything . . .

but I don't *really* care.

They both make brilliant bubble beards

and I know
they're always there.

When I feel sad they make me smile

and they hug me every day.

And if a story scares me . . .

My daddies are amazing –
the world's best **king and king**.

And story time with them will ALWAYS
be my favourite thing!

Goodnight, Daddies.